Book Buddies

Ivy Lost and Found

Cynthia Lord

illustrated by
Stephanie Graegin

CANDLEWICK PRESS

Text copyright © 2021 by Cynthia Lord
Illustrations copyright © 2021 by Stephanie Graegin

First paperback edition 2022

Library of Congress Catalog Card Number 2021946270
ISBN 978-1-5362-1354-6 (hardcover)
ISBN 978-1-5362-2605-8 (paperback)

21 22 23 24 25 26 TRC 10 9 8 7 6 5 4 3 2 1

Printed in Eagan, MN, USA

This book was typeset in Sabon.
The illustrations were created digitally.

Candlewick Press
99 Dover Street
Somerville, Massachusetts 02144

www.candlewick.com

A JUNIOR LIBRARY GUILD SELECTION

To Julia
CL

For my nieces
SG

CHAPTER ONE

Ivy

Ivy's first memory was the birthday party. There was music and bright balloons. A girl's face lit up with joy.

"A doll!" Anne had cried. She cut the strings and untwisted the ties that held Ivy in her store box. "I'll name you Ivy," Anne whispered into Ivy's dark braids.

After that, it was always the two of them: Ivy and Anne.

On warm summer days, Anne played with Ivy outside in the garden. Ivy's tiny blue boots left footprints in the mud.

On gray, rainy afternoons, Anne made new clothes for Ivy. She stitched soft dresses and pants

from scraps of fabric and lace. She made belts from string and rubber bands. She knit sweaters from leftover bits of yarn. Ivy loved them all.

On icy winter nights, snow fell outside the windows. Anne tucked Ivy into blankets and read fairy tales to her. Ivy's favorite part was always "happily ever after."

And every night before she fell asleep, Anne whispered her most secret worries and hopes to Ivy. Ivy always listened.

She never imagined it could change.

As Anne grew up, trips to the garden stopped. Ivy's tiny blue boots stayed clean.

She wore the same white pants and gray sweater for years.

On icy winter nights, Ivy stayed on the shelf. She watched snow fall outside the window while Anne slept.

Missing someone hurts, Ivy thought. *This is how it feels to be forgotten.*

Then one day Ivy was brought to the attic. She was placed in a box with some old clothes.

Ivy went to sleep. Memories came and went, like dreams. Over and over, Ivy remembered the birthday party, the trips to the garden, new clothes, and icy nights, tucked in blankets.

Until one day . . .

The box opened again.

Anne's eyes were older now, but they lit up with joy.

"Ivy!" she cried. "I remember you."

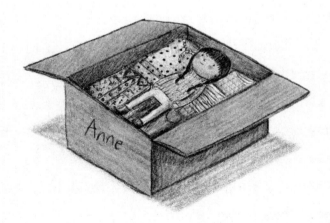

CHAPTER TWO

The Library

Ivy peeked out of Anne's tote bag. Everything was very bright after the dark box. There was so much to see!

There were books on long shelves, in bins, and on bookcases. Shiny posters were on the walls. There was even a shelf of stuffed animals and toys with a sign: BOOK BUDDIES.

Ivy had never seen so many children. Some played games. Some did puzzles at little tables. Others sat in beanbags, listening to their parents read.

"Welcome to the library," Anne called to everyone. "Story time will start in five minutes. Today I'm reading books about bears. Get ready to growl!"

Anne carried Ivy to the Book Buddies shelf. A little girl with pigtails and overalls was patting the toy unicorn's tail.

"Hi, Sophie!" Anne said to the girl. "I have a surprise. I helped my mom clean out her attic yesterday, and look who I found!" She took Ivy from the tote bag. "It's my old doll, Ivy."

Old doll? Ivy's heart broke.

"Today she'll join the Book Buddies," Anne said. "Children can borrow her and read stories to her, like I did."

Ivy didn't want to be borrowed. She wanted to belong to Anne. She wanted to be her favorite toy again.

Sophie smiled. "She can meet the other Book Buddies."

"That's a great idea!" Anne turned Ivy toward a brown bear with a black nose. "Ivy, this is Banjo." Next was a fluffy black-and-white hen with her yellow chick. "Here are Olive and little Roger."

Banjo and Olive looked sweet. Roger had mischief in his eyes. Ivy liked them all.

Homer the owl had brown feathers, fierce yellow eyes, and white tufts on his head. Ivy tried to smile bravely.

"And here's Dazzle!" Sophie pointed to a snow-white unicorn with a sparkly pink tail. "Dazzle is a *boy*," she told Ivy. "He likes stories with magic."

Piper was a gray-and-white flying squirrel. Next to him was a tiny mouse wearing a wool vest and an acorn-cap hat. "That's Marco Polo," Anne said. "He likes to explore."

"And this is Lilyanna. She's my favorite!" Sophie said.

Lilyanna was another doll. She had a gold crown and long sunshine-colored hair. She wore a glittery purple dress with laces up the front.

A princess! Just like in the fairy tales.

"They can be friends," Anne said. "Lilyanna will love having another library doll."

Ivy thought she heard Lilyanna give a tiny sniff, like that wasn't true.

Ivy had always loved her own black braids, little garden boots, homemade pants, and gray sweater. But next to Lilyanna, she felt plain and not even a little bit glittery.

Anne set Ivy gently on the shelf between the hen and the unicorn.

"Come on, Banjo!" Anne picked up the brown bear. "You're the guest of honor at story time today. Our first book is *Brown Bear, Brown Bear, What Do You See?*"

Anne carried Banjo over her shoulder. He smiled back at the other toys.

Ivy wished she could hear the stories, too. Maybe if she closed her eyes and listened really hard . . .

"Are they gone?" a deep voice asked.

CHAPTER THREE

The Toys

The unicorn stretched. "My legs hurt. I've been sitting still for so long," he said in his deep voice.

"I wish Anne would do another *princess* story time," Lilyanna whined. "The last one was at the Valentine's tea party. Anne put me on a special chair. She read fairy tales—"

"Yes, dear. You've told us many times," the hen clucked. "Where are our manners? We have someone new!" Olive put her soft wing around Ivy.

Ivy smiled shyly at Olive. Maybe she could make a friend? Someone to help her understand this new place? Ivy had never had a friend before, except for Anne.

"Whooo are you?" Homer hooted. "What's your story?"

"My story?" Ivy asked.

Piper nodded. "Every toy has a story. I came from a yard sale. Before that, I used to fly through the trees."

"Only when your child threw you," Homer said. "Flying squirrels don't really fly. Not like owls. We fly up. Flying squirrels only fly *down*!"

"I *did* fly," Piper said quietly. "You don't know everything, Homer."

The little mouse tugged on the edge of Ivy's sweater. "I was a Christmas ornament! Anne cut off my string so I could be a real toy. She named me Marco Polo because I'm a brave explorer."

"Anne bought me new for the Valentine's tea party," Lilyanna said. "I'm not an old ornament or a hand-me-down toy."

"Shh," Dazzle said. "I want to hear Ivy's story."

Lilyanna sniffed.

"I was Anne's toy when she was young." Ivy didn't say *favorite toy* because she didn't want to hurt anyone's feelings.

"You must be very old!" Roger peeped.

"Roger, it's not polite to call another toy old," Olive scolded her chick. "Better to say 'well loved.'"

"Tell us about Anne as a child," Dazzle said. "She's always been a grown-up to us."

"I was her birthday present," Ivy began. Then she told them about the clothes Anne had made. She described the trips to the garden. She even told them about the stories Anne had read aloud on icy winter nights, tucked in blankets.

Ivy didn't tell them about being forgotten. It was too sad to remember that. "But that's over now," she said simply.

"Maybe not," Homer said. "I've been tucked in blankets with lots of children since I became a Book Buddy."

Olive nodded. "We're borrowed for two weeks at a time. Roger and I always go together."

"Children play with us and read us stories," Dazzle said.

"I've been to Mexico," Lilyanna bragged. "The family took me on *vacation* with them. I went to the beach and in a hot tub."

"I fell in the toilet once!" Roger said proudly. "The mother dried me with a hair dryer!"

"It was terrifying!" Olive clucked. "Thank goodness the toilet was *clean*!"

"Every borrowing is a new adventure," Piper said. "We each have a journal. The child can draw or write what we did at their house. So our stories keep going and going."

Ivy tried to smile. Borrowing did sound better than being forgotten. It didn't sound as good as belonging to your own child, though.

Maybe these toys had never been loved like that? *Once you've truly belonged, nothing else comes close,* Ivy thought.

"I hope I'm not borrowed by a baby this time," Dazzle said. "The last baby drooled on me. Thank goodness I'm machine washable."

"I hope my next family doesn't have a cat," Marco Polo said. "I was almost swallowed last time!"

"I know Sophie will pick me," Lilyanna said. "I'm her favorite. She said so."

Homer's ears twitched. "Shh, everyone! I hear the children coming. Get back to your places."

"Roger, fluff your fluff!" Olive said. "We want a child to pick us!"

Ivy did not want to be picked. She leaned closer to Dazzle, hoping his big tail would hide her. She wanted to stay at the library. Then Anne would see her every day and remember how much she loved her.

Children came rushing into the room. Ivy peeked out from Dazzle's tail. *Don't pick me,* she wished.

Sophie stopped at the toy shelf with a little boy and an older girl. The little boy grabbed the flying squirrel. "Piper!"

Sophie picked up the princess. "I want to borrow Lilyanna again!" She turned to the older girl beside her. "And look, Fern! A new doll. We can pretend our dolls are sisters. Just like us!"

Ivy heard Lilyanna give a tiny sniff at the word *sisters*.

Fern shook her head. "I don't play with dolls, Sophie."

Whew! Ivy thought. *That was a close call.*

Other children came to the toy shelf. Ivy peeked between the strands of Dazzle's tail. She saw Homer being hugged by a girl. A boy was helping Marco Polo climb the puzzle boxes. Then a girl picked up Dazzle and tucked him under her arm.

Ivy had nowhere to hide.

"Quick!" Sophie grabbed Ivy. "Take her, Fern. Before someone else borrows her!"

Ivy looked into Fern's eyes. *She doesn't want me,* Ivy thought.

"Come on! We have to check out," Sophie said.

Fern sighed and took Ivy.

Ivy was borrowed.

CHAPTER FOUR
Fern

Fern loved both her mom and her dad, but it was hard living in two houses.

At Mom's house, Fern was an only child. She had her own bedroom. She could put her things where she wanted. No one ever took them or moved them. At night her dog, Dusty, slept on the floor beside her bed.

Dad's house was louder and more crowded. After the divorce, Dad had married a woman named Nicole, who already had two children. Sophie was six years old and Ethan was four. Dad lived too far away for Fern to visit every week. So most weeks, Fern talked to Dad on the phone and sent him drawings and photos. But during school vacations and for two weeks in the summer, she came to Dad's house to stay.

When Fern lived with Dad, she shared a room with Sophie. The room was full of Sophie's things. The bottom dresser drawer was supposed to be left empty for Fern. But when Fern opened the drawer to put her things away, it was never empty. There were always notes and drawings from Sophie.

Fern knew that Sophie was trying to be nice, so it didn't feel right to complain. It bothered her, though. Nothing at Dad's was just hers. Not even her drawer.

Fern had to go everywhere with Sophie and Ethan, too. She didn't want to go to the library that morning. Story time was for younger kids, she said. Not for eight-year-olds.

Nicole said she couldn't stay home alone.

So Fern sat in the back with the parents. While Anne read bear stories and the kids sang songs, Fern looked at a library book about fairy houses. It showed how to make them from natural things like sticks, pine cones, rocks, and leaves.

It looked like fun! There were woods around Dad's house. A perfect place to build a fairy house. If she went outdoors quietly, she might escape Sophie and Ethan for a little while, too.

"Can I take this book home?" she whispered to Nicole.

Nicole smiled. "Sure!"

Fern didn't want to borrow a doll, though. She didn't even really like dolls. But when Sophie wanted something, it was hard to say no.

"Fern and I are going to play dolls!" Sophie told Anne as they checked out their toys and books. "I've been waiting for her to come for *weeks*!"

Anne smiled at Fern. "You'll be the first child to borrow Ivy." She scanned the bar code on the fairy-house book and Ivy's small journal. "And I bet Ivy would love a fairy house! She always did like to go outside."

"That's a great idea!" Sophie said. "We can make fairy houses for our dolls. There are lots of sticks and pine cones in the woods."

"How fun!" Anne said. "I'm excited to read about their adventures in their journals."

Fern held the fairy-house book tightly. *I'll wait until Sophie and Ethan are busy,* she thought. *Then I'll sneak outside to build my fairy house by myself.*

"I'm going to make Lilyanna a campsite!" Sophie said as they walked out the door.

CHAPTER FIVE
Outdoors

Ivy hadn't been outside to play in a long time. The sun warmed her hair. The breeze tickled her hands. The pine needles were a soft, sweet-smelling pillow to sit on.

Next to her, Fern had gathered bits of bark, sticks, pine cones, small stones, and other natural things. "The fairy-house book says never use anything that's still growing," she said out loud.

Is Fern talking to me? Ivy wondered. But Fern had said she didn't play with dolls.

For the base of the house, Fern had chosen an oak tree with space between its roots. She added long pine cones to make walls. Pine branches across the top made a roof.

She put Ivy inside.

It smelled like Christmas. Ivy leaned back, remembering. Anne had always wrapped a little Christmas present, just for her. One year Anne knit Ivy a scarf. Another Christmas there was a tea set with tiny plates and cups. The next year there was a small dresser for Ivy's clothes.

"I have a dog named Dusty at my other house," Fern said quietly. "I wish he could come to Dad's house with me, but his fur makes Sophie sneeze."

Fern *was* talking to her! Ivy saw tears in Fern's eyes.

"It's not that I don't like Sophie," Fern said. "She's never mean to me, but I have to share everything with her. It's okay to share the room, but I wish I could have Dad to myself, even just for a few minutes. Sophie gets to have him all the time."

Fern is missing someone, too. Ivy's heart hurt. She wanted to help Fern, but she didn't know how.

"I miss Dusty," Fern said, making a pathway to the fairy house with small stones. "He's a good listener."

I can listen, Ivy thought.

"I don't usually play with dolls," Fern said, "but I like you because—"

Suddenly, a voice rang out. "There you are, Fern! We've been looking for you!"

It was Sophie and Ethan. Fern wiped her eyes quickly.

"You didn't tell us it was time to make the fairy houses!" Sophie said. "I'm going to build

Lilyanna's campsite right next to you! Then our dolls can visit!" She sat Lilyanna on the rock pathway to Fern's fairy house.

"Piper can fly into the trees!" Ethan threw the squirrel high. Piper swished between branches and past leaves. A few acorns fell to the ground.

"Piper is getting food for everyone!" Ethan said happily. He caught Piper coming down. Then Ethan threw Piper even higher into the oak tree.

More acorns fell. This time, Piper didn't come down with them.

"Oh no!" Ethan cried. "He's stuck on a branch!"

"Don't worry," Sophie said. "We can get him down. Just throw something else at him. It will knock him loose."

"Ivy can rescue him!" Ethan grabbed Ivy from the fairy house, bumping the branches off the roof. Pine cones rolled off the walls. He aimed Ivy at the branches.

"Ethan, stop!" Fern cried.

It was too late.

Ivy felt herself soaring upward. Leaves and branches brushed by her. She closed her eyes. *Please let someone catch me!* she wished.

She landed with a thump on something soft. She opened her eyes.

"Hi," Piper said beneath her. "We're in a tree!"

CHAPTER SIX

Forgotten

Ivy looked over Piper's shoulder and down toward the ground. She'd never been so high. If she fell from here, could she break her leg or arm?

Below her, a sparrow jumped from branch to branch. Everything on the ground looked far away and small. The children looked up, but Ivy didn't know if they could even see her between the branches.

"Why do you always have to ruin everything?" Fern snapped at Sophie and Ethan. She
turned and ran for the house.

Sophie ran after her. Ethan followed, yelling,
"I didn't mean to!"

Ivy waited for them to come back.

She waited as the sun sank low in the sky.

She waited as the bats came out of hiding and flew beneath her.

She waited as the crickets started to chirp.

In the dusk, Ivy could barely make out Lilyanna's bright yellow hair on the ground far below them.

Lilyanna would be easy to find, but what about her and Piper?

"Someone will come," Piper said. "The family only gets to borrow us for two weeks. They'll get a notice if we aren't returned on time."

Two weeks felt like forever.

Nothing could be worse than this, Ivy thought.

Then it started to rain.

As night came, Ivy rested her head on Piper's wet fur. What if no one ever came? After a while, her braids would get messy in the wind.

Her clothes would get shabby and faded. Snow would come and cover them both.

She'd never see Anne again.

"When kids throw me, I always come back down," Piper said under her. "This is the first time I've only flown *up*. Thank you for trying to save me, Ivy."

"Thank you for saving me, too," Ivy said. "I might have broken my leg or arm if I hadn't landed on you."

"Soft animals don't break. We can rip, but then someone can sew us up again." Piper sighed. "I'm glad you're here, Ivy. I feel braver with you."

Ivy felt warm inside. She'd never had a toy friend before. If they were forgotten, at least they had each other. "And I feel braver with you, Piper."

Ivy liked that being friends made them both braver. It gave her a brave idea.

"I don't know if anyone will come," Ivy said, "so let's save ourselves."

"How?" Piper asked.

"You're a flying squirrel, right?" Ivy said. "That means you can fly!"

"No," Piper said sadly. "Homer was right. I pretend I can fly, but really, I can only fly *down*."

"Don't you see?" Ivy asked, smiling. "That's perfect!"

"It is?" Piper asked.

Ivy nodded. "*Down* is where we want to go."

CHAPTER SEVEN

Down

Ivy wrapped her arms tightly around Piper's neck. "Ready? Set? Fly!"

Piper pushed off the branch. He spread his legs wide. The skin between his paws stretched to catch the air, like a parachute. "Wheee!"

Ivy kept her eyes open and held on tight. Piper swerved and turned to avoid branches and leaves.

"Wheee!" she said.

They hit the ground with a thump and a bounce.

"Are you okay?" Piper asked.

"No!" Lilyanna whined. "My hair is wet! It has sticks in it! And I'm"—she shivered—"dirty!"

"I meant *Ivy*," Piper said.

Ivy moved her arms and legs. No broken parts! "Yes, I'm okay," she said. "That was amazing!"

"Are you kidding me?" Lilyanna asked. "This is not amazing! It's night. It's raining. We've been *forgotten*." She sniffed. "It's Fern's fault!"

Ivy sniffed back at her. "It is not! Fern and I were just fine until Sophie and Ethan came outside!"

"Fern didn't even want to borrow you," Lilyanna said coldly.

Ivy paused. It was true. Fern hadn't wanted her, and Ivy hadn't wanted to be borrowed. Something had changed, though.

Ivy had liked being played with again. Fern had said, *I don't usually play with dolls, but I like you because—*

Because why?

Ivy really wanted to know.

"I'm sorry," Lilyanna said quietly. "I shouldn't have said that. I've never been forgotten before."

"I have," Ivy said.

Piper and Lilyanna both gasped.

Ivy nodded. "I was forgotten in a box for a very long time. It *was* lonely and sad, but—"

Piper and Lilyanna looked surprised.

But? Ivy couldn't believe she'd said that word, either. Wasn't being forgotten the worst thing that could ever happen?

Being forgotten had been lonely and sad, *but—*

Ivy had made new friends.

A child had played with her again.

She'd had a brave adventure.

She smiled. "Being forgotten means you can be found again."

CHAPTER EIGHT

Found

Overnight the rain stopped. The stars came out. Then Ivy watched the sunrise, pink and gold. It was the most beautiful thing she'd ever seen.

She listened to the birds singing and the squirrels chattering.

She heard the leaves swish high above her in the trees. Ivy closed her eyes and remembered the view from up there.

"I spent the whole night outside, like a real flying squirrel!" Piper said proudly. "We're nighttime animals, you know."

Ivy opened her eyes. "And I saw the world from up in a tree. I'll never forget it!"

They both looked at Lilyanna.

She shrugged. "I got dirty for the first time."

"Really?" Ivy asked, surprised. "Hasn't a child ever played with you in a garden?"

Lilyanna shook her head. "Never."

Ivy felt sorry for her. "Dirt is only on the outside. It doesn't change who you are on the inside," she said. "My boots have been muddy many times. Anne always cleaned them with a wet washcloth."

"I can go in the washing machine. It says so on my tag." Piper showed them. "Machine washable! Then I go around and around in the dryer. It's warm and toasty in there. When I'm done, I'm fluffy and smell sweet."

"Shh!" Lilyanna said. "Someone's coming!"

Then Ivy heard the footsteps, too. It was Fern! Dad walked beside her carrying a big ladder.

"Ivy and Piper! Here they are! How did they get out of the tree?" Fern picked up Ivy. She moved Ivy's arms and legs. "Thank goodness she's not broken!"

"The wind must've blown them down." Dad set the ladder on the ground. "And what's this?"

They both looked at Lilyanna sitting among the scattered pine cones and pine branches that had been Fern's fairy house. Only the stone path was left.

"I just wanted to make a fairy house for Ivy," Fern said. "But Sophie had to make Lilyanna a campsite right next to me, and Ethan threw Piper into the tree. Why do they have to ruin everything? If they had let me play by myself, this wouldn't have happened."

"I know," Dad said. "Sophie and Ethan are just excited that you're here."

"But when we play together, they take over. It's not fair that I have to share everything all the time." Fern looked up at Dad. "The hardest part is sharing *you*. Sophie and Ethan get you every day. I only get you on vacations."

Dad put his arm around Fern. "I'm sorry, honey."

"I miss you," she said, leaning against him.

"I miss you, too," Dad said. "I miss you every day that we're apart. I can see that we need to make a few changes, though. I want you to be happy here."

Fern hugged Dad and he hugged her back.

"I'm glad to know how you feel," Dad said. "Let's think of new ideas to make things better, okay?"

"Okay." Fern saw a movement in the trees. Sophie and Ethan were peeking around a tree trunk. They were trying to hide, but the tree was too small and they were easy to see. Fern giggled because they looked so funny.

"I'm sorry I yelled at you," Fern called to them.

"We just wanted to play with you," Sophie said, coming out from behind the tree.

"I do want to play with you *sometimes*," Fern said. "But other times I like to do things on my own. I'd like you to ask me first."

Sophie and Ethan both nodded.

Fern took a deep breath. It was hard to tell everyone how she felt, but it did make her feel better. "Sophie, I need some things that are only mine—like my drawer. When you put notes in there, I feel like a visitor in your room, not like I belong there."

"Oh," said Sophie. "I wanted to show you I'm happy you're here. I won't do it anymore."

Fern thought about what Dad had said about making things better. "I have a new idea," she said. "Dad, could we get a whiteboard for our room? Sophie could write messages to me there. And I could write messages to her?"

"Yes!" Sophie said.

"That's a wonderful idea," Dad said. "We'll get a whiteboard this week."

"And the fairy house isn't ruined forever,"
Fern said. "It just needs to be put back together."

"We can help with—!" Sophie stopped. She
looked down at the ground. "Can we help?"

Fern smiled. "Yes."

"I can look for some pine branches," Dad said.

"I'll get more rocks!" Ethan said.

"Lilyanna and I will help with the pine cones!" Sophie added. "She's an outdoorsy princess!"

Ivy heard Lilyanna sniff. This time it didn't sound like an unhappy sniff, though.

Ivy looked over at Lilyanna's dirty face. A few pine needles were stuck in her long hair, but her eyes glittered with happy tears.

This will be one of my best memories ever, Ivy thought.

CHAPTER NINE

Just Right

That night, Fern gave Ivy a bubble bath in the sink.

She cleaned Ivy's boots with a warm, wet washcloth.

She brushed and braided Ivy's hair.

Nicole helped Fern use her sewing machine. Together they made a nightgown for Ivy to wear while her sweater and pants were in the washing machine and dryer (with Piper!).

Then Fern tucked Ivy into blankets beside her. Across the room, Sophie tucked Lilyanna into bed with her, too.

Fern opened a book. "Once upon a time," she read aloud, "there was a girl named Cinderella."

As Fern read, Ivy imagined the whole story. She didn't hear Lilyanna sniff once. Not even when Cinderella was dirty from cleaning the fireplace ashes.

Dirt is only on the outside, Ivy thought.

In the middle of the story, Dad came in and listened, too. He waited in the doorway until Fern finished. "And they lived happily ever after."

Then he came in and kissed Sophie and Fern on their foreheads. "Good night, sweethearts. Nicole and I thought we'd all go to the beach tomorrow. Would you like that?"

"Yes!" Sophie said.

Fern nodded. "Can Ivy come, too?"

"Of course." Dad kissed Ivy's tiny forehead. "As long as she doesn't climb any more trees!"

"Ivy does like adventures." Fern laid her cheek on Ivy's head.

Dad smiled. "Fern, I have a new idea. At the beach tomorrow, let's take a little walk together, just you and me."

Fern grinned. "That would be fun."

After Dad turned out the light, Fern said good night to Sophie. "Do you want to bring some buckets tomorrow? We could build a sandcastle for Lilyanna."

"And Ivy!" Sophie said.

Snuggled next to Fern, Ivy remembered. This time, she didn't start with Anne's birthday party.

She remembered the fairy house.

She remembered the view from up in the tree and flying down with Piper.

She remembered a warm bubble bath and listening to a story tucked in blankets with Fern.

Maybe borrowing isn't so bad after all, she thought.

In fact, maybe borrowing was just right.

CHAPTER TEN

Happily Ever After

At the end of two weeks, it was time for Fern to go home to Mom's house. She wanted to see Mom and Dusty, but she knew she'd miss Dad, Nicole, Ethan, Sophie, and Ivy.

It was time for Ivy to go home, too.

At the library, Ethan showed Anne the drawings he'd made in Piper's journal. Piper was flying up and down through the trees. "He was a real flying squirrel!"

"Lilyanna went to the beach!" Sophie showed Anne her drawing of Lilyanna building a sandcastle with Piper and Ivy. "Lilyanna's an outdoorsy princess."

Fern opened Ivy's journal to the first page. "Once upon a time, there was a doll named Ivy," she read aloud. There were stories and pictures of Ivy in the fairy house. Ivy at the beach. Ivy going down the slide at the playground. Ivy climbing the garden vines and listening to Fern read stories. Fern had filled up four pages!

"Nicole and I made Ivy a nightgown," Fern said. "I left it in my drawer for Ivy to wear the next time I'm home at Dad's."

Next time! Ivy liked those words.

"Let me know when you're coming," Anne said. "I'll reserve her for you."

Fern gave Ivy one last hug. "I never much played with dolls, but I like you," she whispered into Ivy's ear, "because you're a good listener and a great friend."

Ivy's heart was full. She didn't even mind being put on the Book Buddies shelf. She was glad to see her toy friends again.

"Story time!" Anne called to the families in the library. "Today I have a surprise. I'm reading books about gardens, and I have a new toy for the Book Buddies shelf. He'll be our special guest today."

A new toy? Everyone tried to peek as Anne pulled something from her tote bag.

Ivy saw a long white beard and a tall, pointy purple hat. "I couldn't resist him!" Anne said. "He's Nugget the garden gnome!"

Ivy smiled as Anne led the families off to story time. She wasn't the new toy anymore. It would be fun to tell Nugget about being borrowed. It might be scary or hard at first, but it was wonderful in the end.

"Are they gone?" Dazzle asked, stretching his legs.

"I had a great borrowing," Marco Polo said. "I drove a toy car and slept in a dollhouse."

"A dog grabbed me," Roger said. "He took me outside!"

"My heart almost exploded with worry!" Olive clucked. "Thank goodness the child found Roger just in time. He was nearly buried!"

Roger nodded. "It was great!"

"I got dirty," Lilyanna said. "Did you know dirt is only on the outside? Mud and sand wash off."

"Ivy and I got stuck in a tree. I rescued us by flying down." Piper smiled proudly at Homer. "Because *down* was where we needed to go."

"And we were forgotten," Lilyanna added quietly.

The other toys gasped.

"Oh my!" Olive covered Roger's ears with her wings. "A toy's worst nightmare!"

"It was awful," Lilyanna agreed. "But then Ivy said being forgotten means you can be found again."

"And we were!" Piper said.

"Wow," Banjo said. "What an adventure!"

Homer nodded. "What did you think of your first borrowing, Ivy?"

Ivy thought for a moment. It *had* been an adventure. Some parts had been hard, but most parts were wonderful.

She didn't know where to begin. So she started at the end. "I think that . . ."

The toys all leaned close to hear.

She grinned. "I can't wait to be borrowed again!"

When story time was over, Ivy didn't hide behind Dazzle's tail. She sat up straight so the children would see her. She wanted them to know that she was a good listener and a great friend. She was not afraid to get her boots dirty. She wanted to be borrowed.

There were lots of empty pages still in her journal—plenty of room for more adventures with other kids. Kids who needed a special friend to play with and read to and listen to them.

Then after each borrowing, she'd come back to Anne and her Book Buddy friends at the library. Over and over.

Happily ever after.

Grab your library card—there's another Book Buddy to check out!

Marco Polo might be a small toy mouse, but he's looking for adventure—if only someone would check him out from the library!

2 **Book Buddies**

Marco Polo Brave Explorer

Newbery Honor winner
CYNTHIA LORD

illustrated by
STEPHANIE GRAEGIN

Available in hardcover and as an e-book

Turn the page for an excerpt!

CHAPTER ONE

Marco Polo

Marco Polo was a mouse Christmas ornament. He was small enough to fit in a pocket and made of soft felt. His tail and arms had wire inside and could be bent to hold things or curled to dangle from a finger or a coat hook.

He wore a little green vest and an acorn-cap hat. A loop of red ribbon was sewn to the back of his vest so he could hang on a Christmas tree.

He had been made for a favorite librarian named Anne.

"Oh my goodness!" Anne said when she saw him. "This little mouse looks ready for an adventure. I'll name him Marco Polo after another brave explorer."

Marco Polo thought a brave explorer sounded like a good thing to be.

At home, Anne looped Marco Polo's ribbon around a branch of her Christmas tree. Every night he watched the tree lights blink: red, green, yellow, pink, and blue. He listened to the Christmas music and happy laughter when people came to visit.

It was a nice life, but not an exciting one.

It's hard to be a brave explorer when you can't go anywhere, Marco Polo thought.

So Marco Polo used his imagination. The Christmas tree smelled like outdoors. He imagined himself in a forest.

He'd race across the deep snow.

He'd go into the darkest middle of the woods.

Wolves and bears might chase him.

But brave explorers are never afraid!

He was just pretending, though. Marco Polo's ribbon kept him tied to the Christmas tree between a snowman and a Santa ornament.

Then on New Year's Day, Anne brought out a big box. She placed it beside the tree.

Marco Polo was excited. *What could be in the box?*

But when Anne opened it, the box was empty.

Anne lifted the snowman ornament off the branch. She cupped her hand to hold it gently. "See you next Christmas," she said, putting the snowman in the box.

Next Christmas? Marco Polo couldn't believe his tiny ears. *What does she mean?*

Anne lifted Marco Polo off the branch. She smiled, holding him in her hand. "You're so cute. I hate to put you away," she said. "If you were bigger, you could be a Book Buddy at the library. The children would love you." Then she sighed. "But you're too small. I'm afraid you'd get lost."

Anne put Marco Polo into the box with the snowman.

Marco Polo's heart broke. *Too small? Aren't mice* supposed *to be small?*

"But . . ." Anne said slowly.

She thought for a moment. Then she got a pair of scissors.

"Sometimes it's good to take a chance," Anne said. She took Marco Polo out of the box. She cut his ribbon.

"You're not a Christmas ornament anymore," she said, pulling the ribbon from his vest. "You're a Book Buddy."

Marco Polo stared at the curl of red ribbon on the floor. He couldn't believe his tiny eyes.

He was a real toy.